BY WILLIAM MATTHEWS

A Happy
Childhood

A Happy Childhood

POEMS BY

William Matthews

An Atlantic Monthly Press Book
LITTLE, BROWN AND COMPANY · BOSTON · TORONTO

LIBRARY OF CONGRESS CATALOG CARD NO. 84–803

FIRST EDITION

COPYRIGHT ACKNOWLEDGMENTS APPEAR ON PAGE 75.

ATLANTIC–LITTLE, BROWN BOOKS
ARE PUBLISHED BY
LITTLE, BROWN AND COMPANY
IN ASSOCIATION WITH
THE ATLANTIC MONTHLY PRESS

HP

Designed by Dede Cummings

*Published simultaneously in Canada
by Little, Brown & Company (Canada) Limited*

PRINTED IN THE UNITED STATES OF AMERICA

for Bill, for Sebastian

*What, should we get rid of our ignorance,
the very substance of our lives, merely in
order to understand one another?*

R. P. BLACKMUR

CONTENTS

A Happy
Childhood

GOOD

I'd seen wallpaper — I had buckaroos all over my
   bedroom — but my friend the only child had ceiling paper;
in the dark he had a flat sky, if stars make

a sky. Six feet above his bed, where the soul hovers
when the body's in doubt, he had a phosphorous
future, a lifetime of good marks for being alone.

He's an only child, you know, my parents would say.

OK, but I slept with no lid, like a shoe left out-
doors or an imaginary friend, with no sky to hold
him down nor light by which to watch him drift away.

Listen, my little mongoose, I know
   the difference between this and love,
for I've had love, and had it taken away.

This feeling-sorry-for-ourselves-but-outward
is one of desire's shiftier shapes:
see how the deep of night is crept upon our love-

making, and how we believe what we disbelieve,
and find in our hopeful arms what we'd thought
to have thrown away, my stolen good,

the map by which we'll part, and love others.

Romantic, you could call him,

since he walks the balance beam
of his obsession like a triumphant
drunk passing a police test;

though, like a man in love
with a woman fools would find plain,
he doesn't turn aside for beauty;

he's a classicist, and studies
nightly a book so persistently good
he can't exhaust it, nor can it him.

Most of the time nothing happens here, we're fond
of saying. I love those stories and poems

an editor for *Scrotum* or *Terrorist Quarterly*
would describe that way, and besides,
every time in all my life I've said or heard

the phrase it's been a good lie, meaning
at least that crime and melodrama rates

are low enough that we can see, if we want,
the huge slow wheel of daily life, love and boredom,
turning deep in the ship-eating waters.

"The whole city of London uses the words *rich*
and *good* as equivalent terms," wrote Wesley
(1788), who failed to include in his whole city
the "honest poor," condemned by such a name
to improve their diet at the cost of honor.

"My good man" means "good for his debts,"
and not for nothing. What better faith
is there for the future than the braid of debt
we make, all of us? The day of reckoning
had better take its time: we're good for it.

I shouldn't pick on myself, but I do:
pimples and scabs and wens, warts, pustules,
the duff of the body sifting out, the dust

and sawdust of the spirit, blotches and slurs

and liver spots, the scar from the dogbite,
the plum-colored birthmark. . . . All this scuff
and tarnish and waste, these shavings

and leavings. . . . Deep in my body the future
is intact, in smolder, in the very bone,
and I dig for it like a dog, good dog.

After a week of sullen heat, the drenched air
bunched as if it needed to sneeze but couldn't,
the sky gives up its grip on itself and — good —

rain swabs the thick air sweet. The body's dirty
windows are flung open, and the spirit squints

out frankly. A kind of wink runs through
the whole failing body, and the spirit begins,

under its breath at first, talking to itself.
Mumbles, snickers, declamations, and next
it's singing loudly into the glistening streets.

Hi Mom, as athletes say on TV,
and here's a grateful hello to my mild

and courageous father. While I'm at it
I'd like to thank my teachers (though

not some — they know who they are) and
my friends, who by loving me freed

my poems from seeking love. Instead
they go their own strange ways

to peculiar moments like this one, when
the heart's good manners are their guide.

THE INTERPRETATION OF DREAMS

What animals dream of I do not know.
  The urchin cat we rented with the house
was sun-stunned one minute and twitched

the next, pursued by humans, maybe.
The valley could be dreaming the haze
that filled it, both it and I

replete, like a wound
cat sleeping. The walled hilltowns
we drove to nights in search

of the perfect pasta also curled
in on themselves, like nutmeats.
How I loved those stone towns,

stark against fire, the houses
rising like tamed bluffs,
fortification as a way of life.

When I imagine an afternoon
nap in Gubbio, let's say, I dream
of light, mild cousin to fire,

bristling its blind rays

like a bottle-brush down house-
facades until they fleck the stony

streetbeds. Then I'd rise and walk
in diminishing circles *al centro*,
where there's a church and a square,

a blare of blank space amidst
all that habit and stricture.
How often I've arrived at myself

like that, as in a dream.
Nothing can be brought to an end
in the unconscious, where

the circuits of self-dramatization
complete themselves endlessly.
The dream-*work*, Freud called it,

"like fire*works* (my italics),
which require hours for their
preparation and then flare up

in a moment." Daydreams like mine
of Gubbio imitate such
condensation and release,

though they lack that umbilical
tether to the other world that makes
dreams art and daydreams gossip.

And daydreams can be broken

off at sluggish will, like mine,
but dreams have their own urgencies.

The other night I dreamed
I was shaking myself awake
beside that waif cat, dead now

for two years. "Let's go to Gubbio
tonight and eat tortellini."
How long it takes to make them right,

and how they flare up
in the mouth like sunspots,
both dense and evanescent.

SYMPATHETIC

In *Throne of Blood*, when they come to kill
Macbeth, the screen goes white. No sound.
It could be that the film has broken,
so some of us look back at the booth,

but it's fog on the screen, and from it,
first in one corner and then in another,
sprigs bristle. The killers close in further —
we're already fogged in by the story —

using pine boughs for camouflage,
and Birnam Forest comes to Dunsinane.
Even in Japanese, tragedy works:
he seems to extrude the arrows

that kill him — he's like a pincushion —,
as if we grew our failures and topples,
as if there were no larger force than will,
as if his life seemed strange to us

until he gave it up, half-king, half-
porcupine. We understand. We too were fooled
by the fog and the pines, and didn't
recognize ourselves, until too late, as killers.

FAT

At first it seemed temporary:
  a ring on the body's bathtub,
a cadet's emblem, baby fat,
something to shuck off as we stride
to work. Now we're used to it

and growing old, we say, swelling
as time thins, and we're a little
proud of it, like an insomniac
who fails to think how a busy
or relentless mind could be

the devil's foundry, or like someone
who talks too much and who's learned
to say so in mid-paragraph.
Fat is likewise deprivation
all piled up, a sort of compound

interest in ourselves,
like a coral colony's.
To the body politic these are
the suburbs and annexations;
soon all of us will be each other

who could as babies put the world
surely to our mouths: some of it
didn't fit, and all the rest
was the self, that paltry wafer,
on which, God bless us, we've waxed fat.

ON A DIET

*Eat all you want
but don't swallow it.*

ARCHIE MOORE

The ruth of soups and balm of sauces
I renounce equally. What Rorschach saw
in ink I find in the buttery frizzle
in the sauté pan, and I leave it behind,
and the sweet peat-smoke tang of bananas,
and cream in clots, and chocolate. I give
away the satisfactions of food and take
desire for food: I'll be traveling light

to the heaven of revisions. Why be
adipose: an expense, etc.,
in a waste, etc.? Something like
the body of the poet's work, with its
pale shadows, begins to pare and replace
the poet's body, and isn't it time?

CONVIVIAL

for Marvin Bell

Four of us sit by a river we can't name
    and don't say how easy it is to say what's wrong
with literary life; we drink Chablis instead.
If the past and future are so important,
St. Augustine blustered, where are they?
They're here. That green at the rim of our gold

Chablis is some vegetal rancor the vintner
couldn't convert to wine, and the cold burrowed
in the riverbed will be smug and slick
and the same cold as long as river slides
over the surface of river here. Longer, maybe,
than talk will foam on these banks, and subside.

It's too easy to talk about everything,
that's what's wrong with literary life:
a novel condensed to a sigh, and death
in a Petri dish. But aren't we those who make
small things well for the joy of it? Say so:
life is sweet. We prove it by letting it go.

WHIPLASH

That month he was broke,
so when the brakes to his car
went sloshy, he let them go.
Next month his mother came
to visit, and out they went
to gawk, to shop, to have something
to do while they talked besides
sitting down like a seminar
to talk. One day soon he'd fix
the brakes, or — as he joked
after nearly bashing a cab
and skidding widdershins
through the intersection
of Viewcrest and Edgecliff —
they'd fix him, one of these
oncoming days. We like
to explain our lives to ourselves,
so many of our fictions
are about causality — chess
problems (where the *?!* after
White's 16th move marks
the beginning of disaster),
insurance policies, box scores,
psychotherapy ("Were your
needs being met in this
relationship?"), readers' guides
to pity and terror —, and about
the possibility that because

aging is relentless, logic too
runs straight and one way only.

By this hope to know how
our disasters almost shatter us,
it would make sense to say
the accident he drove into
the day after his mother left
began the month he was broke.
Though why was he broke?
Because of decisions he'd made
the month before to balance
decisions the month before that,
and so on all the way back
to birth and beyond, for his
mother and father brought
to his life the luck of theirs.

And so when his car one slick day
oversped its dwindling ability
to stop itself and smacked two
parked cars and lightly kissed
another, like a satisfying
billiards shot, and all this action
(so slow in compression and
preparation) exploded so quickly,
it seemed not that his whole life
swam or skidded before him,
but that his whole life was behind
him, like a physical force,
the way a dinosaur's body
was behind its brain and the news
surged up and down its vast
and clumsy spine like an early

15 ॐ

version of the blues; indeed,
indeed, what might he do
but sing, as if to remind himself
by the power of anthem that the body's
disparate and selfish provinces
are connected. And that's how
the police found him, full-throated,
dried blood on his white suit
as if he'd been caught in a rust-
storm, song running back and forth
along his hurt body like the action
of a wave, which is not water,
strictly speaking, but a force
that water welcomes and displays.

BAD

Dew, sweat, grass-prickle, tantrums,

lemonade. One minute summer is all balm
and the next it's boredom and fury,

the library closed, the back yard blandly

familiar. The horizonless summer
recedes with a whoosh on all sides

like air being sucked out of a house

by a tornado, and there in the dead
center stands a child with a crumpling

face, whom somebody soon will call bad.

Beloved of mothers, too good in school and manners
to be true, can this unctuous wimp be real?

He'd be less dangerous if he had no good
at all in him, this level teaspoonful of virtue,

this festoon of fellowship, most likely

to succeed by filling in the blanks and hollows

like a fog or flood. Every morning he counts
his blessings backwards: he's not a crook,

not a recent thief, hates only the despised, and
(here it comes up his throat like a flag) he's not bad.

To pay a bad debt with bad coin, to breathe
bad air between bites (bad bites, an ortho-
dontist would say) of bad food, or worse,
food gone bad. . . .
         By such a token *bad*
means discreditable, that hope is a bad lien
on belief, as if there were no evil but mis-
judgment, bad budgeting,
                     or in the case
of those teeth, bad genes. But let's say it:
evil exists, because choice does, and because
luck does and the rage that is luck's wake.

Here's bad luck for you: on your way to buy
shoelaces you're struck by a would-be suicide
as you pass beneath the Smith Tower. He's saved
and you're maimed, and long after he's released
he comes to visit you in the hospital and you'd

rip his lungs out of his trunk with your poor bare
hands if they'd obey you anymore, though as luck
would have it, they won't. Or, after the operation
cleared out every one of his cancer cells, a new crop
of them blooms along the line of the incision.

All the wrapping paper stuffed into the fireplace
Christmas morning, and all the white and brown
bags, the wax and butcher's paper, the shimmers

and crinkles of spent foil, plastic wrap in shrivels,
the envelopes ripped open 2500 miles away.

And the letters unfolded which are neither true
nor false, bad nor better, but all that the hurt heart

would cook or eat, or give and take. The ghosts
that swirl and stall and dive in the wind
like daunted kites. That we are all old haunts.

The granular fog gives each streetlight
an aura of bright haze, like a rumor:
it blobs as far as it can from its impulse.

The way gossip is truest about who says it,
the world we see is about the way we see;

if this is truth, it's easier than we thought.
What's bad about such truth is needing
to have it, as if it were money or love,

each of which clings to those on whom
enough has long ago, luckily, been spent.

The year I had my impacted wisdom teeth
cracked and tweezered out, I took codeine

for pain and beyond, until a day I could feel
my body faking pain, for which I rewarded it
with codeine. In this exchange the bad

marriage of mind and body was writ large,
and that a good one is work which is work's pay,

and that blame is not an explanation of pain
but a prolonging of pain, and that marriage
isn't a sacrament, although memory is.

When Williams called the tufty, stubbled
ground around the contagious hospital

"the new world," did he mean monumental
Europe was diseased and America needs,
like a fire set against a fire, a home-

made virus? I think so. These may be
the dead, the sick, those gone into rage

and madness, gone bad, but they're our dead
and our sick, and we will slake their lips
with our very hearts if we must, and we must.

THE PSYCHOPATHOLOGY
OF EVERYDAY LIFE

Just as we were amazed to learn
that the skin itself is an organ —
I'd thought it a flexible sack,
always exact — we're stunned
to think the skimpiest mental
event, even forgetting, has meaning.
If one thinks of the sky as scenery,
like photographs of food, one stills it
with that wish and appetite,
but the placid expanse that results
is an illusion. The air is restless
everywhere inside our atmosphere
but the higher and thinner it gets
the less it has to push around
(how else do we see air?) but itself.
It seems that the mind, too,
is like that sky, not shiftless;
and come to think of it, the body
is no slouch at constant commerce,
bicker and haggle, provide and deny.
When we tire of work we should think
how the mind and body relentlessly
work for our living, though since
their labors end in death we greet
their ceaseless fealty with mixed emotions.
Of course the mind must pay attention
to itself, vast sky in the small skull.
In this we like to think we are alone:

evolutionary pride: it's lonely
at the top, self-consciousness. We forget
that the trout isn't beautiful and stupid
but a system of urges that works
even when the trout's small brain is somewhere
else, watching its shadow on the streambed,
maybe, daydreaming of food.
Even when we think we're not,
we're paying attention to everything;
this may be the origin of prayer
(and if we listen to ourselves,
how much in our prayers is well-dressed
complaint, how much we are loneliest Sundays
though whatever we do, say, or forget
is prayer and daily bread):
Doesn't everything mean something?
O God who composed this dense
text, our only beloved planet
— at this point the supplicants look upward —
why have You larded it against our hope
with allusions to itself, and how
can it bear the weight of such
self-reference and such self-ignorance?

TARDY

There's so little of swift time, and what time
we have is so much like held breath, how could
I or anyone be late? Think how fast
the second half of life pays itself out,
faster the smaller it grows, like tape:
how, near the end, the fattened take-up reel
scarcely turns at all. Maybe you've stalled, too,
and dressed your vanity in bandages,
new clothes, and turned your bland back to and left
your mirror, in which you dwindled more the more
you strode away. Did you look back? Tiny
as you were then, how could you be on time,
short steps, short breath? Did you relax and lag?
I did. That's why I'm late. That's why I'm late.

LOYAL

They gave him an overdose
of anesthetic, and its fog
shut down his heart in seconds.
I tried to hold him, but he was
somewhere else. For so much of love
one of the principals is missing,
it's no wonder we confuse love
with longing. Oh I was thick
with both. I wanted my dog
to live forever and while I was
working on impossibilities
I wanted to live forever, too.
I wanted company and to be alone.
I wanted to know how they trash
a stiff ninety-five-pound dog
and I paid them to do it
and not tell me. What else?
I wanted a letter of apology
delivered by decrepit hand,
by someone shattered for each time
I'd had to eat pure pain. I wanted
to weep, not "like a baby,"
in gulps and breath-stretching
howls, but steadily, like an adult,
according to the fiction
that there is work to be done,
and almost inconsolably.

MONDAY MORNING, MONDAY NIGHT

In the dream I woke from I was about
to open some poor wretch's belly with a chain-

saw, a tantrum with an engine.
It's good to hold rage exactly in your

hands, its long blurred snarling loop,
and to feel the blue oily fog of exhaust

in your eyes and nostrils, and watery
fatigue begins to bead on every muscle

in your arms; and not to loosen your pale
tight clamp on the trigger, and to let her rip.

Friday my friend died, whom I love.
They had him hooked to almost every

machine in ICU, as they chummily
called it. They're on a first-name basis

with too much there ("How's Chemo
goin' for ya?") at the hospital, where too much

is their work and office both. Their white clothes

went *whisk, whisk,* and I felt peevish

and childish, not wanting to do their work
nor to be left out from their serious world.

Chuff, chuff: a vaporizer. And the room
dark to save the sight of the measled child.

And tedium like ashes on each muscle. . . .
All the heave and humiliation, the fierce

patience of growing up — it seemed wholly
lost, safe for nostalgia, and here it comes

again, though this time I know how it ends:
I turn away from it, as if it were dying,

and I unplug my love from it, and leave it
to thrill and terror, without a name.

SEATTLE, FEBRUARY

Cold weather and a hard, gray light.
Yesterday a shrill wind that caromed
off the street to punch umbrellas

inside-out, and today a crystalline,
still cold you can't get off your skin,
like city soot, once you're at home,

except by a long, hot, amniotic bath
that clouds the mirror, like memory,
Oh when you were young, you think,

and that's a kind of elegy in itself,
especially if you leave the sentence
and thought incomplete, and the emotion.

Oh when you were young the radio
burbled of shut-ins, and as you let
the screen door slam behind you,

shutting you out, you wondered if you'd
ever be shut in, along with the sick
and prisoners and those who keep them,

along with the lame and crazy, and those
who peer palely from windows like cats
on a rainy day, one smudge in the shadow-

nation of shut-ins, a colony inside

its motherland. Cold outside and warm
in the house, warm in the tub.

Even a short day is long if nothing comes
to an end. Grief comes back and back,
and pleasure teaches us to seek pleasure's

company, but sadness just continues:
it sits in the tub with you and pretends
to listen while you talk to yourself,

explaining, telling some old stories over
and this time getting the details right,
the pace, the tone, the hard, grey light.

MANIC

*I did not know, any longer,
the meaning of my happiness;
it held me unexplained.*

EUDORA WELTY

Out I would go, as if out were a city,
and I was buoyant and self-absorbed,
my own climate, though like a pond
my city held its own warm and chill
districts aloof to the good news and puzzle
of my self. I felt like a child with his first
library card: all bound sadness was my glee.
I thought every book was meant for me,
like a warehouse of pets, and I carried
my special, pled-for limit of six books
per visit like a scepter through the aisles.
Six empty cages. . . . At home I'd line them up
and open the first box of trances
and soon I'd have lived in each one.
I liked to walk as long as it took
to begin to spend attention outside me.
I feel like I'm talking your ear off,
when all I wanted was to describe
one of my walks, like the one that took me
at noon to The Broadway Clock Shop.
Oh I had no ambitions, like a storm,
to be anywhere specific, and then a whole
migration of brass birds left and returned
while I stood there and ignorance
ran up and down my body like a squirrel.

DEPRESSIVE

No wonder it feels like a chore,
   by the hour, the ounce, the follicle,
and no wonder we'd be more bored
without our boring jobs than we are
on the greyest Monday. It's work,
being depressed, and we're tired,
and we fall asleep and dream
and wake like the skim of fat on a broth,
and again work is before us,
in rivulet, in gram, in decibel.
And work is before us in grime,
and in erosion, and in rust.
No wonder we're too busy to rejoice,
unless work is rejoicing,
and indelible, no wonder, the story
of our lives, lumpy with anecdote.

No wonder if we fumble our explanations
of ourselves, like rosaries,
and no wonder we never lose them,
we've saved their lives so many times.
And since sleep doesn't work,
no wonder we mate with ourselves
like this, waiting to see if we
come by, and we do and we go on,
no wonder. For the work of being
depressed is to stay depressed,
the way the work of dreams is to guard

sleep by expanding the fort:
if an alarm should ring the dream
will invent an occasion for bells —
a wedding, a fire, an evening of music,
roll call at the bell foundry —
so that the bells sing out their single
notes, their names, their explanations.

No wonder we love sad songs,
or that when we remember habit
it seems to have been joy itself.
And holidays! The turkey is stuffed
with memories of turkey.
The light seems to come from what's lit,
the way it does in good paintings,
and no wonder. We'll leave our love
for the world where we can, like a dust,
like a prairie of eggs that won't hatch,
a gift too good for us to keep or leave,
and then we'll raise our glasses
just the way we did last year —
a few details are skewed: for extra
credit what's wrong with this picture? —
to its passing, and our own.

A HAPPY CHILDHOOD

> *Babies do not want to hear about*
> *babies; they like to be told of*
> *giants and castles.*
>
> DR. JOHNSON

> *No one keeps a secret so well as a child.*
>
> VICTOR HUGO

My mother stands at the screen door, laughing.
"Out out damn Spot," she commands our silly dog.
I wonder what this means. I rise into adult air

like a hollyhock, I'm so proud to be loved
like this. The air is tight to my nervous body.
I use new clothes and shoes the way the corn-studded

soil around here uses nitrogen, giddily.
Ohio, Ohio, Ohio. Often I sing
to myself all day like a fieldful of August

insects, just things I whisper, really,
a trance in sneakers. I'm learning
to read from my mother and soon I'll go to school.

I hate it when anyone dies or leaves and the air
goes slack around my body and I have to hug myself,
a cloud, an imaginary friend, the stream in the road-

side park. I love to be called for dinner.
Spot goes out and I go in and the lights
in the kitchen go on and the dark,

which also has a body like a cloud's,
leans lightly against the house. Tomorrow
I'll find the sweatstains it left, little grey smudges.

Here's a sky no higher than a streetlamp,
and a stack of morning papers cinched by wire.
It's 4:00 A.M. A stout dog, vaguely beagle,

minces over the dry, fresh-fallen snow;
and here's our sleep-sodden paperboy
with his pliers, his bike, his matronly dog,

his unclouding face set for paper route
like an alarm clock. Here's a memory
in the making, for this could be the morning

he doesn't come home and his parents
two hours later drive his route until
they find him asleep, propped against a streetlamp,

his papers all delivered and his dirty paper-
satchel slack, like an emptied lung,
and he blur-faced and iconic in the morning

air rinsing itself a paler and paler blue
through which a last few dandruff-flecks
of snow meander casually down.

The dog squeaks in out of the dark,
snuffling *me too me too*. And here he goes
home to memory, and to hot chocolate

on which no crinkled skin forms like infant ice,
and to the long and ordinary day,
school, two triumphs and one severe

humiliation on the playground, the past

already growing its scabs, the busride home,
dinner, and evening leading to sleep

like the slide that will spill him out, come June,
into the eye-reddening chlorine waters
of the municipal pool. Here he goes to bed.

Kiss. Kiss. Teeth. Prayers. Dark. Dark.
Here the dog lies down by his bed,
and sighs and farts. Will he always be

this skinny, chicken-bones?
He'll remember like a prayer
how his mother made breakfast for him

every morning before he trudged out
to snip the papers free. Just as
his mother will remember she felt

guilty never to wake up with him
to give him breakfast. It was Cream
of Wheat they always or never had together.

It turns out you are the story of your childhood
and you're under constant revision,
like a lonely folktale whose invisible folks

are all the selves you've been, lifelong,
shadows in fog, grey glimmers at dusk.
And each of these selves had a childhood

it traded for love and grudged to give away,

now lost irretrievably, in storage
like a set of dishes from which no food,

no Cream of Wheat, no rabbit in mustard
sauce, nor even a single raspberry,
can be eaten until the afterlife,

which is only childhood in its last
disguise, all radiance or all humiliation,
and so it is forfeit a final time.

In fact it was awful, you think, or why
should the piecework of grief be endless?
Only because death is, and likewise loss,

which is not awful, but only breathtaking.
There's no truth about your childhood,
though there's a story, yours to tend,

like a fire or garden. Make it a good one,
since you'll have to live it out, and all
its revisions, so long as you all shall live,

for they shall be gathered to your deathbed,
and they'll have known to what you and they
would come, and this one time they'll weep for you.

The map in the shopping center has an X
signed "you are here." A dream is like that.
In a dream you are never eighty, though

you may risk death by other means:
you're on a ledge and memory calls you
to jump, but a deft cop talks you in

to a small, bright room, and snickers.
And in a dream, you're everyone somewhat,
but not wholly. I think I know how that

works: for twenty-one years I had a father
and then I became a father, replacing him
but not really. Soon my sons will be fathers.

Surely, that's what middle-aged means,
being father and son to sons and father.
That a male has only one mother is another

story, told wherever men weep wholly.
Though nobody's replaced. In one dream
I'm leading a rope of children to safety,

through a snowy farm. The farmer comes out
and I have to throw snowballs well to him
so we may pass. Even dreaming, I know

he's my father, at ease in his catcher's
squat, and that the dream has revived
to us both an old unspoken fantasy:

we're a battery. I'm young, I'm brash,
I don't know how to pitch but I can

throw a lamb chop past a wolf. And he

can handle pitchers and control a game.
I look to him for a sign. I'd nod
for anything. The damn thing is hard to grip

without seams, and I don't rely only
on my live, young arm, but throw by all
the body I can get behind it, and it fluffs

toward him no faster than the snow
in the dream drifts down. Nothing
takes forever, but I know what the phrase

means. The children grow more cold
and hungry and cruel to each other
the longer the ball's in the air, and it begins

to melt. By the time it gets to him we'll be
our waking ages, and each of us is himself
alone, and we all join hands and go.

Toward dawn, rain explodes on the tin roof
like popcorn. The pale light is streaked by grey
and that green you see just under the surface

of water, a shimmer more than a color.
Time to dive back into sleep, as if into
happiness, that neglected discipline. . . .

In those sixth-grade book reports
you had to say if the book was optimistic
or not, and everyone looked at you

the same way: how would he turn out?
He rolls in his sleep like an otter.
Uncle Ed has a neck so fat it's funny,

and on the way to work he pries the cap
off a Pepsi. Damn rain didn't cool one weary
thing for long; it's gonna be a cooker.

The boy sleeps with a thin chain of sweat
on his upper lip, as if waking itself,
becoming explicit, were hard work.

Who knows if he's happy or not?
A child is all the tools a child has,
growing up, who makes what he can.

ALICE ZENO TALKING,
AND HER SON GEORGE LEWIS THE
JAZZ CLARINETIST IN ATTENDANCE

*Now if all of you were gone
I could sing those songs in a row
without stopping, but since you're here
they've all flown out of my head
like that many birds.* It makes her
so happy to say this she won't laugh.
She began in Creole French and didn't
switch to English until her son came in,
sixty, in a rumpled suit, and sat,
his long-fingered hands not so much at rest
in his lap as asleep. *I believe I know
this genneman here.* Her interviewer's glad
to drop his paltry French and Ft. Wayne
accent. There's whisper and scuffle
and somebody goes out for Cokes.
*My great-grandmother came over
from Senegal when she was eight,
and her mother's name was Zaire.*
She hovers a second at *great* to get
the number of generations right.
Some of the songs go back that far.
This is great stuff, her interviewers
think — they're folklorists — but she
means something else. "Are any
of those songs about slavery?" *No,
actually, but a lot of them
are about freedom.* They're trying

to link her to a theory of the past.
Creole? Creole born from here.
Silence. They can be heard riffling
for a next question, and it's about
a song to which she knows and recites
the words. Her voice is low, as usual.
Her son's trumpeter for years, Kid
Howard, seldom played above the staff —
that was George-domain up there,
and George wound his loops and kerf
around the melody the band
had to tend so George could
curl and twine. The great Baptist hymns
he played straight as a Catholic boy,
ever a good guest to the earth, could arrange.
Even those hymns he played sexy,
she used to think but never say.
And isn't the clarinet strait as the gate?
That rain-soft tone, but urgent enough. . . .
In the low register the clarinet
can make you shiver and ripple
with goosebumps and can send
its breath-drenched messages
through arms and legs that show
no passing force inside or out, but hum
like telephone wires in wind.
I'm so old I can't remember a lot
and every day now I'm glad for,
I give something away the chirrun
will need later on. It's chirrun
the music is for, that's what I say.
George doesn't speak on this topic
but thinks how music is not to forget,

that music is about time
and not to be afraid of it,
but to deliver by hand raw meat
to the lion's mouth, and to praise
what is fearful. George shifts in his chair.
"Can you sing that song you just said
the lyrics to?" the interviewer asks.
A pause. *I did.* "No, Mama," says George,
and his voice could be drying a dish
after a holiday meal, "you didn't sing
it, you spoke it." *I did*, she says, and means
that's that. More silence. Love's been
keeping time all along and comes in on the beat,
explicit. She's loved that boy for sixty
years, and his brother, too. *Gracious knows*
I used to sing sing sing those boys
to sleep when they were only babies.

ARROGANT

The person I fear most in the last two rounds is me.

TOM WATSON, *leader after two rounds in the 1977 Masters, at a press conference*

Watson is tired and doggedly polite.
One reporter asks a question so
routine and cynical he's disgusted
by himself, and then jots down the answer.
What kind of job is this for a grown man?
he wonders, and so does Watson, who worked
most of his memorable life to be here
and now can't tell if he wanted more
to be excellent or famous. *If this be
fame, bring me excellence.* Nobody moves.
He who would win had best begin to learn
his part. "I'll take one last question," he says,
and they give it to him, and he tells them
what they need to hear to go away
and what he needs to say to fall asleep
and dream hypnotically of practice,
the dew-trails balls leave on the green early
mornings, the bright rage happiness burns by
when what you love is yours and yours alone.

CIVILIZATION AND ITS DISCONTENTS

*Integration in, or adaptation to, a human
community appears as a scarcely avoidable
condition which must be fullfilled before
[our] aim of happiness can be achieved.
If it could be done without that condition, it would perhaps be preferable.*

FREUD

How much of the great poetry
of solitude in the woods is one
long cadenza on the sadness

of civilization, and how much
thought on beaches, between drowsing
and sleep, along the borders,

between one place and another,
as if such poise were home to us?
On the far side of these woods, stew,

gelatinous from cracked lamb shanks,
is being ladled into bowls, and
a family scuffs its chairs close

to an inherited table.
Maybe there's wine, maybe not. We don't
know because our thoughts are with

the great sad soul in the woods again.
We suppose that even now
some poignant speck of litter

borne by the river of psychic murmur

has been grafted by the brooding soul
to a beloved piece of music,

and that from the general plaint
a shape is about to be made, though
maybe not: we can't see into

the soul the way we can into
that cottage where now they're done with food
until next meal. Here's what I think:

the soul in the woods is not alone.
All he came there to leave behind
is in him, like a garrison

in a conquered city. When he goes
back to it, and goes gratefully
because it's nearly time for dinner,

he will be entering himself,
though when he faced the woods,
from the road, that's what he thought then, too.

PRURIENT

Suppose the past could be surprised,
like Pompeii the morning after:
the uncomposed dead, their pets
heraldic in duty to habit,
uneaten food in its batter of lava.

Is any human instant true,
as museums imply, allegiant
to the dead and their belongings?
What puzzle would we leave if now,
just now, some vast disaster snuffed

us all but left our interrupted
daily lives, half-open drawers?
That's what the curse of the mummy
is: that we break our privacy
with pounding hearts and find

another ignorance, like a doll
inside a doll. *I can't let you in,*
a haggard voice explains, *the place
is haunted.* We ask, *By whom?* The voice
replies, *By you.* And in we go.

SENTIMENTAL

I admire tinsel as much as gold: indeed,
the poetry of tinsel is even greater,
because it is sadder.

FLAUBERT

For breakfast, loss, and day has just begun
to shuffle the cards of its weather, though
by now weather is only an emblem
of loss to us; we have our emotions

at the ready for lunch, which is the food
of childhood on a bed of summer lawn
lit by the last instant before Mother
called us in for dinner, which, then as now,

turns out to be leftover loss in sauce.
Beautiful Mother in the doorframe
calling us across the lawns and alleys
and fields rich in itch-inducing weeds,

preserve our losses, that we never starve,
not before bed nor the next morning,
nor for lunch, nor for dinner, nor even
in memory, where you call us always home.

METICULOUS

*I have passed the age of boredom and I
left part of myself with it.*

FLAUBERT

The blare of blank paper: the solace
of making lists, tracking fresh snow.
The list grows. How busy I must be.

To have planned a day is almost
to have lived it. *Here*, I stab it
again, where I crossed out a near

disaster, and I let my voice
trail off, three dots, the last bootprints . . .
What became of him, I wonder,

rapt and lost, who was almost me?

FAMILIAL

W hen the kitchen is lit by lilacs
        and everyone's list is crumpled or forgot,
when love seems to work without plans

and to use, like an anthill, all its frenetic
extra energy, then we all hold,
like a mugful of cooling tea,

my grandmother's advice: *Don't ever
grow old*. But I'm disobedient
to the end, eager to have overcome

something, to be laved by this light,
to have gone to the heaven of grown-ups
even if my body cracks and sputters

and my young heart grows too thick.
I want my place in line, the way
each word in this genial chatter

has its place. That's why we call it
grammar school, where we learn to behave.
I understand why everyone wants

to go up to heaven, to rise,

like a ship through a curriculum
of locks, into the eternal light

of talk after dinner. What I don't
understand is why one would balk to die
if death were entry to such heaven.

WE SHALL ALL BE BORN AGAIN BUT
WE SHALL NOT ALL BE SAVED

"We're going," the paramedics said
        (how I burned to be part of that *we*),
"to take you to the hospital."
It would be life as a direct object
for a while. Into the ambulance
they slid me like a loaf of bread.

There would be tests, I understood,
to see why my heart beat in triplets,
and I could see it myself, on TV,
an hour in the afternoon like a soap
opera. Echo-cardiogram, they
called it. "Narcissus, is there someone

else?" I watched my eager heart
lash and batter for an hour, only
its normal violence, an intern assured
me, but she came back and back
abnormally to see me: "Can I listen
to your heart?" I couldn't trust her.

My green heart on TV looked violent.
This would be an inside job.
Who could break one of those but itself?
It's never been that we *have* bodies:

we *are* bodies. I had to trundle
a kind of aluminum coatrack

along the hall just to pee, because
of the IV, and I had to eat essence
of junket, and nurses brought me pills
in little paper thimbles. This balm
of obedience and stupor, I thought
while I vomited blood, is all

my docile study. I'd been too sick to take
my own side in a fight, but against whom?
Another day I'd learn the obvious,
that it was me, but that's another story.
In this one I'm untethered from my
machines, my mild, green-faced flock,

and can walk around weakly on my own,
can pack my bags and pills and go out
into Boston safe to die some other day.
"How will this change your life?"
My heart will push me along like a good
rhythm section. I plan to notice everything.

RIGHT

We always talked about getting it right,
    and finally, by making it smaller and smaller,
like inept diamond cutters, we did. We chiseled
love's radiant play and refraction

to a problem in tact and solved it
by an exact and mannerly contempt,

by the arrogance of severity,
by stubble, by silence, by grudge,
by mistaking sensibility for form,
by giving ourselves up to be right.

You have the right to be silent, blank
    as an unminted coin, sullen or joyfully

fierce, how would we know? What's truly yours
you'll learn irremediably from prison.

You have the right to clamp your eyes shut,
not to assent nor to eat nor to use our only

toilet in your turn, but to hold your breath
and frail body like secrets, and to turn blue

and to be beautiful briefly to yourself.
And we have our rights, too, which you can guess.

There's fan belts stiffening out back for cars
they haven't made in fifteen years, but if one
of them geezer wagons wobbles in here, we got

the right fan belt for it. We got a regular
cat with a fight-crimped ear and a yawn pinker
than cotton candy in fluorescent light, and we

got the oldest rotating Shell sign on Route 17;
hell, we're a museum. You can get halfway
from here to days beyond recall, and the last

half you never had a chance at, from the start.

Too right, my son accuses me when I correct
his grammar, but then, like an anaconda
digesting a piglet and stunned by how much blood
he needs to get this one thing done, he pales,

and then he's gone, slipped totally inside
himself, someplace I can't get from here
or anywhere, and now I need to tease him out
from his torpid sulk, or to wait till he slithers

out on his own. Come to think of it, that's how
I got here, eager, willful, approximate.

Four months of his life a man spends shaving,
a third of it asleep or pacing his room in want
of the civil wilderness of sleep, like a zoo lion

surveying the domain of its metabolism,
and what slice of his life does he pass

mincing shallots, who loves cooking?
If time is money, it's inherited
wealth, a relic worn smooth and then

worn to nothing by pilgrims' kisses,
and there's no right way to keep or spend it.

Right as rain you are, rain that shrivels
the grapes and then plumps the raisins.
You were right when you felt peeled,
like a crab in moult, and right you were

when you chafed stiffly against your shell

and wanted out. You're condemned to be right,
to agonize with what's right as the future
invades you and to explain the inevitable
past as it leaves you to colonize yourself,

to be you, finally to stand up for your rights.

Gauche, sinister, but finally harmless because
flaky, somehow miswired, a southpaw

(there's no more a northpaw than there is a soft-
nosed realist: the curse and blazon of rectitude
is that even the jokes about you are dull,

and your fire is embers and cozy, grey at the edge
and pink in the middle, like a well-cooked steak),

a figure of fun, as someone outnumbered so often
is, and all because you bring me, and you're right,
my irresistible self, hand outstretched, in the mirror.

On the way to the rink one fog- and sleep-thick
morning we got the word *fuck* spat at us,

my sister fluffed for figure skating and I in pads
for hockey. The slash of casual violence in it
befuddled me, and when I asked my parents
I got a long, strained lecture on married love.

Have I remembered this right? The past is lost
to memory. Under the Zamboni's slathering tongue
the ice is opaque and thick. Family life is easy.
You just push off into heartbreak and go on your nerve.

THE THEME OF THE THREE CASKETS

Men and women are two locked caskets,
each of which contains the key to the other.

ISAK DINESEN

One gold, one silver, one lead: who thinks
this test easy has already flunked.

Or, you have three daughters, two humming-
birds and the youngest, Cordelia, a grackle.

And here's Cinderella, the ash-princess.
Three guesses, three wishes, three strikes and

you're out. You've been practicing for this
for years, jumping rope, counting out,

learning to waltz, games and puzzles,
tests and chores. And work, in which strain

and ease fill and drain the body like air
having its way with the lungs. And now?

Your palms are mossy with sweat.
The more you think the less you understand.

It's your only life you must choose, daily.

Freud, father of psychoanalysis,
the study of self-deception and survival,
saw the wish-fulfillment in this theme:

that we can choose death and make what we can't

refuse a trophy to self-knowledge, grey,
malleable, dense with low tensile strength

and poisonous in every compound.
And that a vote for death elects love.
If death is the mother of love (Freud wrote

more, and more lovingly, on mothers
than on fathers), she is also the mother
of envy and gossip and spite, and she

loves her children equally. It isn't mom
who folds us finally in her arms,
and it is we who are elected.

Is love the reward, or the test itself?

That kind of thought speeds our swift lives
along. The August air is stale in

the slack leaves, and a new moon thin
as a fingernail-paring tilts orange

and low in the rusty sky, and the city
is thick with trysts and spats,

and the banked blue fires of TV sets,

and the anger and depression that bead

on the body like an acid dew when it's hot.
Tonight it seems that love is what's

missing, the better half. But think
with your body: not to be dead is to be

sexual, vivid, tender and harsh, a riot
of mixed feelings, and able to choose.

CHARMING

Because language dreams in metaphors,
charm is always like something else,
like luck, or wealth, or like a tune
to whistle while coaxing soup
from chicken bones and two turnips.

Because ice is like stone, though once
it was water, and because kissed ice
means blue lips, charm needs to know
the names of distress and remedy,
and what words are not spoken, and when.

Because charm is an argument
about politics, that it works best
for the rich, and about magic,
that it works best for those who recant
politics, charm is warily polite.

And because charm is like love,
the way ice is like water, charm
tends its investment and dreams
when it sleeps, and wakes hungry,
as if from exacting work.

And because to fly in a dream is fierce
pleasure, charm wakes with a kind word.
It's important to start in the right place,

like a child possessed of a story.
First the witch, then the snow, and then

the starling-throng like a blizzard
of shameful thoughts, and then winter:
ice to kiss and the right names
in the right order, the sexual secret
of spring's coming back at all.

Though spring is all burgeon and broadcast,
a tosspurse, survival's brash manners,
because charm dwindles and hoards,
because charm repeats, because charm
will save itself before it remembers us.

RESTLESS

Reflected light wrinkles the bay.
It's late, and tomorrow sloshes
onto the pebbly beach and out again.
Eventually the familiar
melancholy of travel over-
comes its novelty, and we pack again.

But first, in some far place, we speak
plain things to ourselves in italics —
we mean them — about the heart and home.
Surrounded on three sides by water,
we belong at last to the continent.
That's what we came here for, the talk

and seething water, and what swells in the pauses
as talk slackens. That vigilant
God we prayed to keep us while we slept,
long years ago, has shattered to each of us.
Some dream of travel, some of home.
None dreams blank water or pure light.

MASTERFUL

They say you can't think and hit at the same time,
but they're wrong: you think with your body, and the whole

wave of impact surges patiently through you
into your wrists, into your bat, and meets the ball

as if this exact and violent tryst had been a fevered
secret for a week. The wrists "break," as the batting

coaches like to say, but what they do is give away
their power, spend themselves, and the ball benefits.

When Ted Williams took— we should say "gave" —
batting practice, he'd stand in and chant to himself

"My name is Ted Fucking Ballgame and I'm the best
fucking hitter in baseball," and he was, jubilantly

grim, lining them out pitch after pitch, crouching
and uncoiling from the sweet ferocity of excellence.

THE HUMMER

First he drew a strike zone
   on the toolshed door, and then
he battered against it all summer
a balding tennis ball, wetted
in a puddle he tended under
an outdoor faucet: that way
he could see, at first, exactly
where each pitch struck.
Late in the game the door
was solidly blotched and
calling the corners was fierce
enough moral work for any
man he might grow up to be.
His stark rules made it hard
to win, and made him finish
any game he started, no matter
if he'd lost it early.
Some days he pitched
six games, the last in dusk,
in tears, in rage, in the blue
blackening joy of obsession.
If he could have been also
the batter, he would have been,
trying to stay alive. Twenty-
seven deaths a game and all
of them his. For a real game

the time it takes is listed
in the box score, the obituary.
What he loved was mowing
them down. Thwap. Thwap.
Then one thwap low and outside.
And finally the hummer.
It made him grunt to throw it,
as if he'd tried to hold it
back, but it escaped. Thwap.

AN ELEGY FOR BOB MARLEY

In an elegy for a musician,
  one talks a lot about music,
which is a way to think about time
instead of death or Marley,

and isn't poetry itself about time?
But death is about death and not time.
Surely the real fuel for elegy
is anger to be mortal.

No wonder Marley sang so often
of an ever-arriving future, that verb tense
invented by religion and political rage.
Soon come. Readiness is all,

and not enough. From the urinous
dust and sodden torpor
of Trenchtown, from the fruitpeels
and imprecations, from cunning,

from truculence, from the luck
to be alive, however, cruelly,
Marley made a brave music —
a rebel music, he called it,

though music calls us together,

however briefly — and a fortune.
One is supposed to praise the dead
in elegies for leaving us their songs,

though they had no choice; nor could
the dead bury the dead if we could pay
them to. This is something else we can't
control, another loss, which is, as someone

said in hope of consolation,
only temporary, though the same phrase
could be used of our lives and bodies
and all that we hope survives them.

WRONG

There's some wrong that can't be salved,
something irreversible besides aging.

This salt, like a light in the wound it rankles. . . .
It seems the wound might exist to uncover
the salt, the anger, the petulance we hoard

cell by cell, treasure the body can bury.
As J. Paul Getty knew, the meek will

inherit the earth, but not the mineral rights.
And what's our love for the future but greed,
who can't let go the unbearable past?

By itself *wrong* spreads nearly five pages
in the *OED*, and meant in its ancestral forms
curved, bent, the rib of a ship — neither
straight, nor true, but apt for its work.

The heart's full cargo is so immense it's not

hard to feel the weight of the word
shift, and we might as well admit it's easy
to think of the spites and treacheries
and worse the poised word had to bear

lest some poor heart break unexplained, inept.

It's wrong to sleep late and wake like a fog,
  and to start each paragraph of a letter with *I*,

and wrong to be cruel to others, the swarms
of others damp from their mutual exhaltations,

and wrong to complain more than once
if others are cruel to you, wrong to be lonely,

to come home in spirals and not to unscrew
but to whistle and twist by yourself like a seed

which the wind will know how to carry
and the wind will know when to drop.

It's too quiet out there. There's something wrong.
  I smell a rat. You can't fire me, I quit, the boss
will never pay enough, it's so hot in here I think

I'll take off my job. Then I ripped off her dress, then
I hit her, I was like a wild man, except I was ashamed.

I've read about creeps in the papers, they hear voices
and don't disobey. I don't obey one, not even me,

and I'm all of my voices. Creeps, I said, and Creeps,
I sang, but I'm one. So are you. Let me buy you a beer.
I'll bet you're full of good stories. Let me buy you another.

Even in sleep, the world is smaller. In a dream
I want you to go somewhere with me, and you
won't come. When I wake there's fog at the waists

of the trees, like a sash. There are treetops
and treetrunks, and a smear where the two don't
join. It's wrong to be in this much pain. The bay
is out there somewhere. Yes. I can hear someone

singing badly over the waters. No. It's a radio
with a cracked speaker drilling through the fog,
faithfully towing a lobsterboat to its traps.

Maybe what's wrong, if *wrong* is the right word,
is that we like to think the body is defending us,
as if when some part of the world gets in you
that shouldn't, you're done for, and so

your antibodies run wild and do not stop
when the work they're designed for is done,

but they rage against the very body. What
little I know of the mind, I know it sometimes
works like that, if *works* is the right word,
and it is. Not the body, nor the mind, has a boss.

What's wrong is to live by correction, to be good
for a living — proofreader, inspector of public works —,

to go into the tunnels of error like a rat terrier
and come out and know you will be fed for it.
Sop, mash, some dark velvety food rich as bogbottom,

some archival soup with one of every nutrient,
an unbearably dense Babel of foodstuffs, what you get

for knowing wrong when you see it, for knowing
what to do next and doing it well, for eating
the food and knowing there is nothing wrong with it.

Corms and bulbs into the ground, bone meal
buried with them like a pharaoh's retainers,
and an exact scatter of bark on top for mulch. . . .

And the rank weeds winter down there, too,
as if the mulch were strewn for them, as if
diligent worms broke ground for them; and who's

to say, turning this soil, that they're wrong?
The detection of wrong and the study of error
are lonely chores; though who is wrong by himself,

and who is by himself except in error?

NOTES

"Alice Zeno Talking, and Her Son George Lewis the Jazz Clarinetist in Attendance":

Based on tapes of Alice Zeno in the Tulane University Jazz Archives.

"Civilization and Its Discontents":

In Beyond the Pleasure Principle *Freud wrote that "civilization obtains mastery over the individual's dangerous desire for aggression by weakening and disarming it, and by setting up an agency within him to watch over it, like a garrison in a conquered city." The garrison metaphor recurs in* Civilization and Its Discontents.

ACKNOWLEDGMENTS

Some of these poems first appeared in the following magazines:

AMERICAN POETRY REVIEW: "Dew, sweat . . . ," "All the wrapping paper . . . ," "When Williams called . . . ," "I'd seen wallpaper — . . . ," "Romantic, you could call . . . ," "After a week of . . . ," "We always talked about . . . ," "You have the right to be silent . . . ," "There's fan belts . . . ," "It's wrong to sleep late . . . ," "Corms and bulbs . . ."

ANTAEUS: *Civilization and Its Discontents, The Interpretation of Dreams, The Psychopathology of Everyday Life*

THE ATLANTIC MONTHLY: *Charming,* "Listen, my little mongoose . . . ," "It turns out you are . . . ," *Loyal, Whiplash*

BLACK WARRIOR REVIEW: "My mother stands . . ."

BLUEFISH: "The granular fog . . ."

CHOWDER REVIEW: *Fat*

COLUMBIA REVIEW: "The map in the shopping center . . . ," *Familial*

CRAZY HORSE: *An Elegy for Bob Marley*

GEORGIA REVIEW: "Beloved of mothers . . . ," "To pay a bad debt . . . ," "Here's bad luck . . . ," "The year I had my impacted . . . ," "Most of the time . . . ," "The whole city of London . . . ," "I shouldn't pick on . . . ," "Hi, Mom . . ."

IOWA REVIEW: *The Theme of the Three Caskets*